I

UNTIL SUNSET

A Cycle's Journey to Freedom

Saavanna Satheesan

To Madiha Ma'am

CONTENTS

PREFACE

Dear Reader,

Thank you for choosing to read this book! My name is Saavanna Satheesan. If you're wondering why this book was written, here's how it all began.

During one of my classes with my most favorite teacher, we were told to do an activity of making poems or stories or anything innovative on the environment. Me being a small poetess myself, I had a compilation of poems related to that already. When I presented that to my teacher, she started lecturing me about how good I was at writing and encouraged me to use my talents to write a book. That could've been the only time I would have ever paid attention to a lecture! Every single word she said was absorbed into my brain. I then promised her that one day I would write a book and show it to her. Almost 6 months later, after publishing an e-book, when we were doing another activity, I told her that I started working on writing this book. And she asked 'Who? About me?'. Co-incidentally I also needed a female character in this book when she said this. I then made her a second promise that I would make her that said character (who is also the heroine of this book). So, you see, if that teacher hadn't lectured me about all those things 9 months earlier, then you wouldn't probably even be reading this book right now.

It just reminds me of this wonderful quote I read- "A good teacher is like a candle- it consumes itself to light the way for others." They go through so many sleepless nights and loads of stress and pressure to do something for us. And that should be appreciated.

This book is fully dedicated to my teacher, the one who inspired me to write this book, taught me important moral values, realize my own talents, and moreover helped me go after my dreams. The most charming, kind , amiable and understanding teacher in this whole-wide world- Madiha ma'am.

I hope you all love reading this book as much as I did, writing it.

Happy Reading!!

Yours truly
Saavanna Satheesan

THE BEGINNING

I still can't figure out why. I keep thinking but still can't find an answer. I mean, why would you abandon someone just because of the weather?

It's been months since I have moved. Hummer and I have been

stuck here for ages. Hummer has almost given up hope now. I would too, but I still have a feeling things are about to change.

I remember the time when I was first created, from the factory to the shop. What most people don't know is that every single part of the cycle has a different soul. When put together, all the souls combine to form one big head. For me, I'd say I'm extraordinary. I had my metal and tires shipped from the U.S! Although, my paint and screws were coming from the local store a couple of meters away from the building I am currently living in. After my parts were gathered and fixed, I was placed in a room filled with other cycles. The only problem was that that

room was filled with cycles pro-
duced a couple of weeks earlier.
And to prevent dust from covering
them up, they were capped with
plastic which made it practically
impossible for them to talk. Unlike
humans, we don't require oxygen
to breathe or survive. As long as
we are pumped with air, we can go
riding for miles and spend a normal life talking with other cycles.
But the only thing that can per-
haps kill us, is 'Rust'. So, when I
was placed in that room, I didn't
feel excited at all.

I spent most of my time staring at
the walls trying to figure out what

kind of paint they were painted with. And soon, I too was covered in plastic. I felt suffocated then. Several weeks had passed, when I was put into a truck that was to go to a cycle shop in a market nearby. Within hours we arrived at the shop. The man who owned the shop was very kind enough to throw the plastic off me. I could finally breathe fresh air! Wait, didn't I say we don't need to breathe?

◆ ◆ ◆

So, I spent almost a whole month waiting in that shop for someone to pick me. I wouldn't say that the sales were high. It was in the mid of June when the door was opened by a young lad along with his sister and his father. They came inside and started going through the cycles one by one. Almost instantaneously, the boy ran over to me, held me by the handle, and said, "Daddy! Daddy! I want this one! It looks so beautiful." I giggled. I liked how innocent the boy was. He was careful with his words. His father examined me while his sister was staring at another cycle. Soon I was out of that shop in a car on the way 'Home'.

We drove past many streets and finally approached a cluster of buildings. Once they parked, they took me out and inside the building. It was a peach one, with its paint slightly wared off because of rain and dust. We went in the elevator and came out facing a door, which I supposed was their home and my new home.

The flat looked astonishing. The walls were well decorated, and the place was adequately furnished. They went to a corner in their bedroom which had a wall-size window and placed me there. And that's where I still sit today.

Like I said earlier, I've been sitting here for eons now. Humans have evolved so much that they have lost feelings for us, non-living objects. What baffles me, even more, is the fact that they call us non-living. What do they think? That we can't feel? That we can't speak? Or are we just too invisible for them to even notice? Every single object that they call non-living has a voice, has life, and has emotions.

But they can't just seem to figure it out for some arbitrary reason. I mean, there is no point in whining about this now for they can't hear us even if we yell.

A STRANGE DREAM

It was 9 pm. I was starting to feel sluggish. The girl and the boy were already in bed, snoring loud while their parents were preparing to go to bed. I was gazing out of the window. I watched the Moon as it gleamed among the stars. The next moment the lights were off. Hummer was sleeping like everyone else. I stared out one last time before my eyes went shut. I could see myself riding through a dark cave. It seemed to be going on forever. Suddenly, my vision started getting misty. A beam of light swept across my eyes. I appeared in a strange land.

The hills and the grass were painted blue, pink, and purple, the sky- yellow. The sun, well I couldn't seem to find one. I was amazed. I mean, have you ever seen land as strange as this before? Obviously, no. And there was no way for me to escape because number one, I was conscious I was in a dream and I couldn't wake up until it ended and number two, there was a huge black wall behind me. So, I had no choice but to explore this new place. I drove ahead.

I came to a small town. There were people, vehicles, and animals all around. It was very noisy altogether. But I felt most of the noise was coming from a hospital nearby. And written on top was, 'Fairview Hospital, Tillydrone.' So that is what this place

is called! Weird as it was, cars

and bikes were driving in through the main entrance! So, I too drove inside. The hospital looked much huger on the inside than the outside. Nurses were roaming around, and people were talking to doctors in their rooms and so much more! I went to the main deck. There was a billboard stuck up with the names of doctors and why you should consider talking to them.

'Dr. McKenzie Issac Barnes- For Life Problems', I read. Well, that sounds like someone I need to visit. I decided to meet her. There was a drive-through for vehicles. I went in and booked an appointment with her and got myself a token. After some time, I heard my token number being called to Room 27. I drove all the way there.

I was right behind the door. I was scared but all the same, I pushed the door open with my wheels and went inside. I saw a lady sitting on a table nearby. She looked gorgeous.
She turned over to me and said, "Oh, hello there Mr. Yahoo! How are you?"
I was confused. I mean even

if I replied, would she be able
to hear me? Like I said earlier,
humans can't seem to hear
us, non-living objects.
"New here, I suppose? If you're still
wondering whether I will be able
to hear you or not, well let me tell
you, in the land of Tillydrone, anything and everything is possible.
So speak out!" she said.
"Oh, I didn't know that,"
I stammered.
"It's alright, anyways," she
said, "My name is McKenzie,
how may I assist you?"
"Well, I heard that I could
consult you for life problems."
"Yup, that's correct!"
"Uh, well, you see my
LIFE is a problem."
"And how is that so?"

And so, I told her my life story from start to finish. She listened attentively. In the end, I highlighted my problems once again.

"In my world, people call us non-living which hurts our feelings. Plus, the family I live with hasn't even let me move till now. It's only in dreams like this wherein I DREAM of moving around. Basically, what I am trying to say is, I want to be allowed to move freely without anyone to stop me."

"I see, so would you want to know a way of escaping from where you stay?" said McKenzie.

"Yes," I said.

She got up and picked up a book nearby. It looked like it had almost a thousand pages. She flipped through some pages.

"Let me tell you something. I used to work in the Prodigy School of Tillydrone before. So the reason I became such a doctor was because in that school, we spend our time connecting with our students and teaching them valuable life lessons. So, I try to talk to my patients and solve their problems the same way I did to my students before. But in your case, you need a plan to get something that you want. I think you need to talk to Professor Quintin Harrell."

"Okay, so I'll just book an appointment with him. Thank-"
"You won't be able to book an appointment."
"Why not?" I asked, perplexed.
"Professor Quintin passed away five years ago."

"Oh dear, then I shan't be able to meet him," I said sadly.
"But fortunately for you, in Tillydrone anything and everything is possible. We have specially made time machines that can help you meet him."
"And never return I suppose," I muttered to myself.
McKenzie narrowed her eyes on me and raised an eyebrow.

"You see, that is your problem. You're hopeless. Where there's a will, there's a way. Always remember that. We have been sending patients to travel back into the past and meet Professor Quintin ever since he was gone. So, we know

what we are doing. I'll book an appointment with him for you."
"You just said I won't be able to!"
"Must I repeat myself? In the town of Tillydrone, nothing is impossible. We have special phones that can call a person from the past. And I said YOU won't be able to book it, I can because I have the phone."

Phones that can call back into the past! You must be joking with me! How's that practically even possible? Oh well, as long as I get to meet Professor Quintin, I am ready to do anything, even if it's crazy.

◆ ◆ ◆

SHE LOOKS SO FAMILIAR...

It was daybreak. I was still brooding about the dream I had when the children's father came up into the room toting in a brand-new study table and a spinning chair. I guess it belonged to the girl for I heard her squeaking in joy behind him. He placed the table and chair next to the wall I sit. The table wasn't fancy and so was the chair. They both were just plain, ordinary black. I don't get why it's something to squeak about!

The girl then came running in with her brand-new laptop, which was black again and sat on the chair to attend her online classes. It worked the same way as her real classes. She had to join the meetings from 7:40 in the morning to 1:50 in the afternoon. Since I had nothing else to do, I chose to watch her classes until it was done.

She first had a small 10-minute period for her attendance and then gradually all the other subject periods would start. She had math first. Her math teacher seemed to be a very jolly one, cracking jokes now and then. I watched her as she solved problem after problem. I guess math isn't a fun subject to learn after all. Next, she had English. And then she had all other periods one by one until it came to the very last period, social studies. Her teacher looked beautiful. She was teaching them about latitudes and longitudes. It sounded so boring. So, I continued to admire her teacher's face. I couldn't read her name for the letters were way too small. I think the first letter was M.... or was it N?

Her eyes were charming while her silky hair hung from head onto her neck. Her face reminded me of forget me not's. Her face was just so- wait a second, have I seen her before? Her face looks so familiar. Or maybe not. I must still be slumberous.

As soon as her classes got over, she jumped on the bed, stretched out her hands and legs, and laid down on the pillow with her blanket. No sooner had she done that, I heard her mom yell at her. Well, I suppose all moms would be mad if they did that, wouldn't they?

I started thinking about my dream all over again. A small sense of regret came over me because I was going to be visiting Professor Quintin Harrell who was to tell me a way of escaping my own 'Home', and when I was in the cycle shop all I wanted was someone to carry me home. I was starting to rue my decision. Maybe I should not leave? Maybe after the summer season is over, they might take me out.

But I should do what I want to. I want to be free. So, I think I did make the right decision after all.

And I think meeting McKenzie was worth it and- wait, MCKENZIE!

She's the girl's social studies teacher! Yes, I am sure, 100%! But how is it possible that I saw her teacher in my dreams when today was the first time I saw her? Now that's odd. Well, we can find out tonight.

After watching a movie, like they always do every weekend, the family was ready to go to bed. The next moment the lights were off. I thought about the dream I had, stayed focused on it, and closed my eyes, hoping to fall into the same dream. And I did!

I landed at the entrance of the hospital. It was very busy today. There were a lot of nurses crowded in Dr. Fire Cracker's room. When I asked one of the staff why was it so crowded, he replied giggling, "Mr. Rhys Evans had 5 rounds of beans non-stop apparently, and his body can't seem to stop producing weird noises every second." I chuckled too. Well too bad for him!

I went to the reception and got myself an appointment with McKenzie.

I was then told to wait for she was busy with another patient. So, I waited in their parking lot, watching out for my token number to be called.

THE MEETING

After a couple of minutes, I was called into her room. "Ah yes, Mr. Yahoo, how are you?" she asked.

"Oh, I'm fine, thank you," I said back politely.

"Just give me a minute-KAMILA!"

"Who is she?"

"Oh, Kamila Adams? She's my assistant/waitress," McKenzie said.

Just then Kamila rushed inside the room.

"I'm really sorry, I almost forgot it's time for your next meal, forgive me. Oh, do tell me what you want to eat," she said.

"For the appetizer, I would like to have an Ice Walnuts & Fruit Salad. For my main course, I would like a Deep-Fried Star Retriever, a Stir-Fried Grim Cassowary, Bunyip Buns, Planar Garlic & Lime Crumble, Breaded Salt Prawn, and Stewed Fluffy Molly along with Jackalope Yogurt."

I never knew that McKenzie had such a big appetite! She paused for a moment to think about dessert and then she continued, "Okay for dessert I would *LOVE* to have Spark Cranberry Ice Cream, Volcanic Almonds & Avocado Fruitcake, Griffin Fudge, Flame Northern-Style Cookies, and a slice of Gudriocket Cake."

She's definitely going to get a sweet

tooth after this! When I thought she was finally done with her order she said, "And I would like to have Harmony Sweet & Spicy Milk for my drink," with a smile.

There was a moment of silence as she finished. Kamila stared into her eyes, and she stared back into Kamila's pale face, smiling. I thought Kamila was used to this, but I guess she wasn't.

"Oh, I better get going then,"
Kamila said almost trembling.
McKenzie turned her face
over to me and said, "Now
where were we? Ah, yes. I

have booked an appointment with Professor Quintin at 4:30 IPT for you, tomorrow."

"IPT?"

"Into Past Time. Now the entire process is going to take about two hours. One for preparation and the other for traveling through the time machine. You must be in the hospital at sharp 2:27. In the next three minutes, you will be escorted to the preparation room. Once the preparation is done, you will be permitted to enter the time machine. So, how does that sound?"

"Good but there's a slight problem. You see, the time I go to bed in my world differs day to day. Some days I sleep super late or some days super early. All this depends on when the family turns off the light and goes to bed. And if I am not mistaken, the time in Tillydrone and my world is the same. So, if I go to bed around nine then how in the world will I be able to reach here at 2:27 in the afternoon?"

"Well, that is not exactly my problem. Maybe you could try sleeping early. And remember this is not my need, it's yours. So, you are responsible for it."

◆ ◆ ◆

THE PREPARATION

It was dawn. I woke up tense. Yes, it was my need and obviously, I was the one responsible for it but how in the world was I supposed to fall asleep in the afternoon when the sun's still shining in my eyes?

As the clock ticked into the afternoon, I began getting worried. I decided that I would start preparing myself to go to sleep at 2:25. So, hopefully within the next two minutes, I might be able to fall asleep.

When it was 2:25, I began. I closed

my eyes and condensed hard and thought of the hospital. But it was difficult. With the girl squealing like a mouse in the background, the T.V on, the boy on a call-things were getting convoluted. I was jumping through the hopes! I started to feel like I was spinning around in the air. Finally, I landed on solid ground. When I opened my eyes, I was at the hospital. I can't believe it worked! I quickly rushed inside the hospital and checked the clock. Only a minute had passed! I immediately ran to the reception.

 "Um, can I book an appointment with Dr. McKenzie please?"

"Reason?"

"She had told me that I need to be here at sharp 2:27 to travel back in time to meet

Professor Quinton Harrell."

"Oh, why didn't you tell me that sooner? Come with me, you only have a minute left before the procedure starts!"

She then guided me to a room at the back of the hospital.

It was humongous! There were machines and robots of all sorts that were roaming around. But what fascinated me the most was this enormous rectangular box covered with something that looked almost like seaweed and spiders and a billion other insects!

"Slimming on the passenger please!" yelled the lady

So many nurses ran towards me with buckets filled with some greenish slime. They formed a circle around me with almost a meter's distance from me.

"Um, what do you mean by this slimming-"

No sooner had I uttered those words, they dumped the whole thing over me. EWWWWW!

It smelled like rotten fish!

"Okay the first part of the *preparation* is done," she said.

"Wait- so what's the second part?" I asked tensed. Were they going to cover me in feathers? Or maybe some sand? I didn't want to look like a monkey in front of everybody!

"Oh don't worry sir, you just need to let that dry now and then you can meet Quintin," she assured me.

And so I waited for almost an hour covered in green rotten slime. I honestly felt very weird having that all over me. I felt cold and sticky all at the same time. After a while, the lady came back to me and asked, "So its about time. Are you stressed?"

"Not really," I replied back.

"WELL YOU SHOULD! If there's even a teeny-weeny misplacement of wire or a faulty part in the time machine, oh boy, you're going to be more than just doomed!" she said back.

I was astonished. I mean, wasn't it her job to relieve my stress? Well, if you ask me, SHE'S NOT HELPING.

But what happened next was even more shocking. Remember, that huge rectangular box I was talking about earlier? THAT WAS THE TIME-MACHINE! Even though it looked like an old piece of junk, that was it!

I was made to stand in front of the box. Then they switched off the lights of the room. It was completely dark. My heart was pounding. It was like a horror movie- well, almost. Close by was a control panel which was through which they would apparently turn on the time machine. A nurse clicked a red button on it, and then a blue light shone from the time machine and into my eyes. When I tried to focus on it, I could see the entire UNIVERSE! How the stars glittered in the darkness that dwelt across! It looked mesmerizing.

"Now listen up, we don't want you to end yourself in a mess. When your time travelling, you're going back to the past. It's not something easy as you think it is nor was it easy to build this either. When you go through this machine, you're not just going back to the past, you're going to experience it again in the form of memories. As you fly across the machine, you'll be able to see memories of you and someone else floating beside you like a cloud. They'll look enticing to experience again but remember, NO MATTER WHAT DO NOT TURN TOWARDS IT! Those are all the evil spirits that come to hypnotize you. So be careful. You'll know when your destination arrives for there will be a white door that awaits you at the end of the journey. Good luck!" the lady said.

I don't know if I had paid attention to all of THAT but oh well, I guess some or the other way, I'll land safe and sound. I looked one last time at all the nurses, who were staring at me. Then I looked back at the receptionist. She nodded. I turned towards the time machine. I could hear my heart pounding loud, I held my breath and without turning back, I went into the time-machine.

MAKING THE PLAN

As soon as I rode in, I felt weightless. I felt light as a feather floating through and across space. Surrounding me was millions and trillions of stars. And just like the receptionist had said, there were these cloud-like things that showed some of the sweetest memories I had.

But there was some that caught my attention. There was one in which the children's father was riding me to the supermarket. I remember that. It was fun to ride through the breeze. There was another one, in the park where the girl was riding me.

There was another one where the boy was riding me and so much more. But I don't know what was making me feel so emotional, but I was starting to want to go into the cloud. I could experience those fun times all over again.

I could spend time with the girl and the boy and their parents once more. I could feel what it was to be with them. Just as I was about to step inside the cloud, I heard a voice yell behind me, " NO, DON'T!"

I spun around. I couldn't believe it, it was MCKENZIE!

"McKenzie, but I thought-"

"Yes, I know. But I thought I might as well just come along with you. I mean, it's been long time since I visited Professor Quintin. So yeah."

"Oh that's nice. At least I won't feel lonely. Hey, wait- isn't that the white door?"

A pale white door seemed to be fading in near one of those clouds.

"Let's go through it," I said. And so, we did.

We landed in this room that was

a real mess. There were papers pinned all over the dark green walls and some lying on the floor. There was a huge bookshelf with books that looked ancient which had spider-webs at almost every corner! And at the end of this shabby room was an old table, an old chair and some more ancient, torn, and shabby books piled on top of the table. On the chair sitting was a man who looked almost in his late 40's wearing a suite.

"Ah yes McKenzie, How are you?" he said in a deep voice.

"I'm fine, thank you. How about you?"

"I'm doing great. Oh, and that must be Mr. Yahoo"

And so we chit chatted a little before he asked-

"So, what is the problem, and how can I help?"

So I had to tell the problem all over again and how McKenzie told me that I could request him to make me a plan to escape from where I currently live.

"Hmm, I see.. For the time being, I don't have a plan. If you could give me a couple minutes time, I might be able to come up with something."

"But, where can we go?" I asked for we or *at least I* was new to this place.

"There's a coffee shop just down by the street. You could have a sip and come back," he suggested.

And so McKenzie and I found ourselves in *Sip'n Munch Coffee Shop* a few moments later. Obviously, I can't drink coffee. I didn't even know it was a drink until I saw McKenzie sipping it! Meanwhile, I stared outside the shop and onto the streets. Tillydrone looked way different then than it did in the *future*. Whilst I admired the land, McKenzie had finished her coffee. So, we decided to go back to Quintin's office. It was in this building opposite to a store.

When we reached, he began explaining what he had come up with.

"My idea is pretty simple but complex at the same time. You know that it's only in dream lands like Tillydrone where even objects like you can speak, move, and be heard. But in real world it is not. Now I don't know where you want to escape off too, and I will let that stay as your decision, but I can help you to move and roam around in the real world-"

"Wait, is that even possible?" I questioned him.

"Yes, it is. By casting a spell on you that can let you move in any place in the entire universe. In dreams or in the real world."

"Oh then that's great! You can just cast it on me right now and be done with –"

"No, I cannot."

"Huh?"

"This is the difficult and most complex part. If you think about it, I am casting a spell on you in your *DREAM* that must let you move in the real world. And this cannot be performed casily. It requires a lot of skill and effort."

"So what are you trying to say?" I asked.

"I am trying to say that I need something in return."

"If it's money that you want, I'm broke."

"Not money."

"Then?"

"A sacrifice."

"A what-"

"A sacrifice. A sacrifice made from a person who knows you, loves you, ready to do anything for you and who exists in Tillydrone."

I was stunned. I asked, "Uh- when you say sacrifice, what exactly do you want the person to sacrifice? And how will that help to cast that spell?"

"I believe, that if another force is present while casting the spell on you, it can help make it more effective. There's an endless pit at the back of my office. The person will have to jump inside it. Once they do, I will get a bit of their power that will help me complete my spell."

"Uh, will they be able to come back afterwards?" I stammered.

Whoever was going to that for me, I didn't want them to like PERMANENTLY just go.

"Sadly, no," said the Professor.

THE SACRIFICE

I was appalled. I didn't know what to think or speak.

"Um Professor, do you mind if I like come back tomorrow, or time-travel back and decide?"

"Yahoo, you cannot go back just like that. Unless signals are steady and they make sure there are no faulty wiring, we can't time travel back again. That's why we give our patients only one chance to travel back in time. So, you must decide here and now," McKenzie said.

"Okay then," I stuttered, "I'll decide and I will come back, Professor."

Me and McKenzie went outside and

onto some grass on the side of the road.

"I feel like I'm in a dilemma right now, McKenzie. I don't know anyone who loves me, or who's ready to do anything for me."

A breeze blew as I wondered what to do. It was very quiet. No cars, no honking. Just me and McKenzie.

All of a sudden, McKenzie sighed and said, "Maybe I could do it. I can make the sacrifice for you. I mean, I do love you and I know you so…."

"Wait, do you really mean what you just said?" I asked, feeling more shocked.

"Yeah."

I looked at her eyes. I could make out that she was dead-serious about it. But, she's such a nice person that I didn't want to loose her.

"I think we can find out another person."

"Yahoo, there's no time for another person to know you properly. This is your chance to get what you want. Just use me," she said.

I almost felt paralyzed at this point.

"So?" she asked.

"Okay, I guess," I said shakily.

Without even looking back she started walking back to Quintin's office. I followed her. I was speechless. I really admired her courage to do something for someone. Soon we were in his office.

"Decided yet?" he asked.

"I am going to sacrifice for her," McKenzie said, boldly.

Quintin smiled back at her.

He then told us to wait a bit so that he could get everything set.

As soon as he left, I turned to McKenzie.

"I-I wanted to know if there's some

way, I can repay you. I don't know how or if that is possible but," I said, almost in tears.

She turned over to me, kneeled down and said," You know Yahoo, I really do love you. I understand what you're going through but let me tell you, in today's world, a sacrifice is never paid."

And she smiled.

I honestly didn't know what to say, I felt clueless. Just to imagine that in the next few moments this woman was to disappear before my eyes for something I wanted. I highly respected this woman. It was only a few days before that I came to know of her. But to think that very person is going to sacrifice for me before my very own eyes, it's just so- it's a feeling that

I couldn't express. A person who's ready to sacrifice one's own self for someone else meant that they loved that person dearly. I felt like tearing up.

"McKenzie, there's something I wanted to ask you."

"What is it?" she asked me, smiling.

"Ar-are you a social studies teacher? I mean like the girl who's living with me, her teacher looked like you."

She chuckled a bit and said, " I am surprised you figured that out. I'm also a normal person living on Earth, but I ended up finding this place called Tillydrone and started working in my sleep! Remember when I first met you, I said I worked as a teacher before? I meant the same thing." She winked at me and smiled.

I COULDN'T BELIEVE WHAT SHE JUST SAID. But before I could say anything more, Quintin called us into the room.

At the center of the room was a deep, black, and endless hole with walls like a well.

"As soon as I get what I need, you need to stand near me so that I can chant it on you, alright?" Quintin asked."

I agreed. I watched as McKenzie slowly walked towards the well. My heart was pounding so fast.

She put her feet on the edge of the well and look at me. I murmured a low *'Thank you'* 'under my breath. McKenzie smiled and nodded to Quintin. He nodded back. She looked at me one last time and jumped. My heart must have missed a beat. I started shedding tears for the first time in my life. So what if it rusted me up? That woman just something even greater than that. A second later after she jumped, I heard a painful scream.

It echoed past my ears. I could hear my heart beats in my ear. I was crying my tears out. *"Noooooooooo-ooooooooooo,"* I yelled, *"McKenzieee-eeeeeeeeeeeeeeeeeee."*

I wish I could have done something for her. I felt regretful. Just for the sake of my wish, a woman had to sacrifice herself. I felt so bad.

FREEDOM, AT LAST...

Iwas crying out bitterly. I felt like everything was my fault. I could see through my tears, that a white puff of something floated out of the well. I stared at it sniffing. The professor started murmuring some enchantments in Spanish. It sounded like this:

Oh estrellas y luna
(O' stars and moon)
Oh sol y nubes
(O' sun and clouds)
Otorgar libarted
(Grant freedom)
A esto ciclo nuestro

(to this cycle of ours)

Sniffing still, I went near Quintin. He started swaying his hands over me with the white puff being tossed from one hand to another. He finally swung his hands all around me and dropped the white puff onto me. Almost instantaneously I was lifted into the air and spun around at intense speed. I then landed on the ground again.

"The spell's been placed on you. It can be used only one time. So, make use of it as much as you can. If you keep sniffing about McKenzie's sacrifice nothing's going to happen. She did it for a cause, remember that. And wherever you want to escape off to, you'll have to wait *UNTIL SUNSET* because the spell will only get activated after it. You're good to go now. Hopefully, we'll meet again. Someday, sometime."

The next moment I appeared back into the real world, in the corner where I've been placed.

When I looked at the time, it was nearing sunset! Only 2 more hours! I just had to wait until sunset and then I would be free!

I was wondering where I should go. Maybe I could travel the world. But where should I start? I could begin at the park nearby.

As time flied by, it was nearing sunset. The evening sun cast long shadows on the ground. The slanting rays of the sun gave a warm orange tinge to the sky.

And you wouldn't believe it, but the family was going out to the theatres to watch a movie called *Spider Man: No Way Home* ! So, whilst they're chillin' and eating popcorn I would have escaped out of this house and into the paradise I've dreamed of.

And so, after the family left, I prepared to leave. I told my final goodbyes to Hummer.

"I sure will miss you, dude. And here's some advice. Don't wait to get placed in some cycle shop. Now that you've got the opportunity to spend life, use it well. Go chase those dreams of yours to travel the world. Because in the long run, you're not going to regret it."

I thanked him.

I was curious if the spell worked, so I tried to move to and fro in the same spot, and it worked!

Quiet as a mouse I drove to the front door. I lifted one of my wheels and pressed down the handle. Luckily it wasn't locked! So, I moved my back wheel back and opened the door. I drove into the corridor and used my handle to click onto the button to take the elevator. I went down, opened the main entrance door, and stepped onto the road.

As soon as I touched my front wheel on the road, a strong breeze blew. The whole world seemed unnaturally dark, as if it had been drained of all light. I drove a bit and reached the entrance of the park. There was lush and verdant grass everywhere with trees growing here and there. In the center stood a lonely path with a couple street lamps. I stared into the sky. The pale moon shone like a silvery claw in the night sky as I looked up at the blanket of stars that stretched to infinity. It almost seemed as if the moon was smiling at me with a great big smile like McKenzie's. I smiled back. Without that one woman's sacrifice, I wouldn't be standing where I was today. I took a deep breath. It was now or never. I rode into the darkness that stretched on for many more years to come.

ACKNOWLEDGEMENT

Writing a story is hard. Just to write the starting line itself takes almost an hour. When I was writing this book, I couldn't seem decide how to start-off. My head just went blank and I couldn't seem to be able to think of anything! I laid on the bed, tossed around for almost 1 to 2 hours before I fell asleep. The next day, though, it wasn't the same case. I had people who helped me, motivated me and inspired me to write the book. And you wouldn't believe it, but I managed to finish 2 chapters just like that because of them! I would like to thank :-

My father- *For suggesting ideas*

My brother and my mother - *For supporting me*

and most of all,

My teacher- *For motivating me with her inspiring words.*

ABOUT THE AUTHOR

Saavanna Ayyappath Satheesan

Saavanna Satheesan, a young teen-age girl has penned many kids stories and poems from a small age. She posts them regularly on her blog - Sometimes I Wonder...
She is loved and appreciated by her family and

friends alike for her pleasing work. She has not won any awards just yet but aims to win one soon. She also hopes to be an inspiration for all young minds out there.
You can follow her at:
https://wonderstories101.blogspot.com